A DAY WITH Wilbur Robinson

by WILLIAM JOYCE

who also produced the film adaptation
known as *Meet the Robinsons*
while snapping his fingers in the air

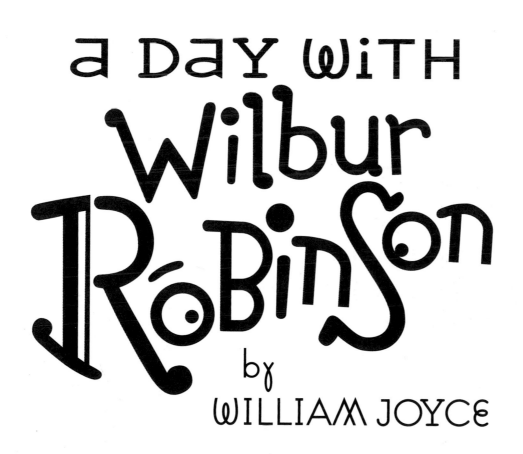

a Day with
Wilbur
RoBinSon

by
William Joyce

Atheneum Books for Young Readers
New York London Toronto Sydney New Delhi

I'd like you to meet the Robinsons.

Wilbur Robinson is my best friend, and his house

is the **GREATEST** place to visit.

i walked up and said hello to the twin uncles, Dmitri and Spike. As always, Wilbur opened the door just before I knocked.

"Come on in," he said. "Lefty will take your bag."

it's kind of dull around here today," said Wilbur.

I looked around. Aunt Billie was playing with her train set, Cousin Pete was walking the cats, and Uncle Gaston sat comfortably in the family cannon.

"Your dad needs you out in the backyard!" he shouted as he blasted himself across the room.

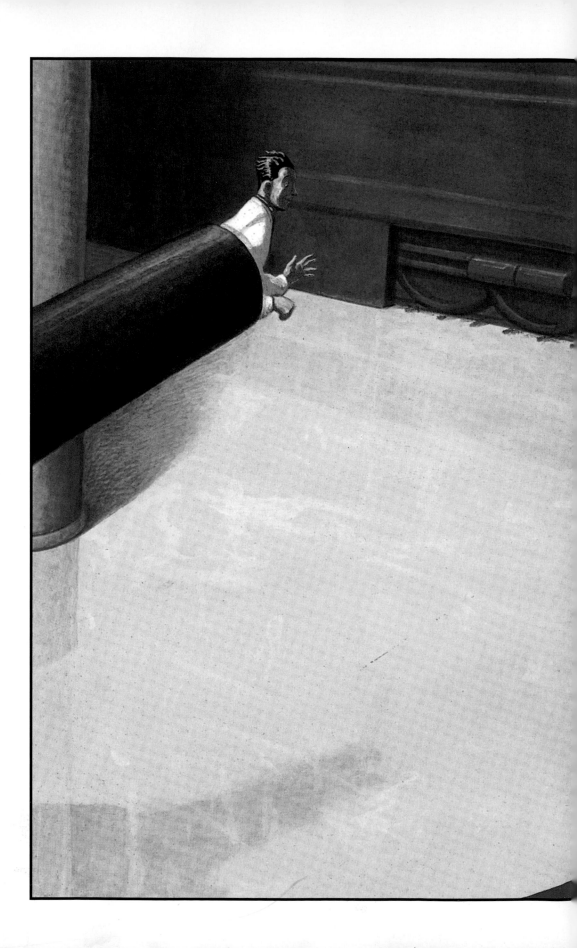

In the backyard, we found Mr. and Mrs. Robinson and their robot, Carl. They were scouring the lawn with the matter detector.

"We're looking for Grandfather's false teeth," Mr. Robinson explained. "Of course, we haven't seen *Grandfather* lately either," he added. "Could you boys go and ask around?"

We asked Uncle Wormly if he'd seen Grandfather's teeth, but he was busy with a new friend. One of his bugs suggested we check out back. The photon elevator was busted, so we took the stairs.

I don't remember the weather report mentioning snow for the east wing," yelped Wilbur.

After helping Uncle Nimbus with his new snowball shooting device, we searched on but found neither Grandfather nor his teeth.

None of the lab equipment had seen a thing.

But Uncle Orbley popped by to lend a hand.

"Ask Uncle Judlow," he gurgled. "He knows

everything!"

We found Uncle Judlow, relaxing with his brain augmentor.

"It helps him think deep thoughts," Wilbur whispered.

"'Mississippi' spelled with Os instead of Is would be 'Mossossoppo'!" blurted Uncle Judlow.

"See? What did I tell you?" Wilbur exclaimed.

"Have you seen Grandfather Robinson's false teeth?" I asked.

Uncle Judlow blinked. "They're wherever he left them," he answered after some thought.

In the den, Wilbur's sister Tallulah was talking on the phone and eating grapes. His other sister Blanche was modeling her new prom dress.

"Do the shoes match?" she asked.

"They're swell," we chimed.

"Have you seen Grandfather Robinson's false teeth?" I asked.

"Or Grandfather?" asked Wilbur.

"Not lately," said Blanche.

Yawning, Tallulah shook her head and ate another grape.

Somebody had left the Time Machine on, so the dinosaurs were at their usual spot by the pool.

"Jeez, I hope Grandfather didn't get lost in the Mesozoic period again," said Wilbur.

"That'll definitely make him late for dinner," I said.

"We're striking out," said Wilbur, discouraged. "And I'm hungry, so let's eat."

Cousin Laszlo came by to demonstrate his new antigravity device.

"Have you seen Grandfather Robinson's false teeth?" I asked.

"Nope, but I bet they're floating around here someplace," mused Cousin Laszlo.

Suddenly, the faint, familiar strains of "Potato Head Blues" came wafting from the house.

that's it!" yelled Wilbur. "It's Friday—Grandfather's in his lab working with his dancing frog band!"

We rushed to the lab. Sure enough, there was Grandfather with his friends Mr. Ellington and Mr. Armstrong. Grandmother Robinson was helping.

"Have you found your teeth, Grandfather?" shouted Wilbur over the music.

"Nah, haven't theen 'em." He smiled.

"I guess we'll just keep looking," I volunteered.

"Thure do apprethiate it," said Grandfather as the music played on.

We found Grandfather!" Wilbur announced as we ran outside.

"Good work!" said Mr. Robinson. "Now if we could only find those teeth!"

"Last time I was here, we were looking for your grandfather's glass eye," I reminded Wilbur as we walked.

"Yeah, he's always missing a part," Wilbur admitted.

"Ahoy!" called Uncle Art, newly arrived from abroad. "Looking for a lost bit of Grandfather? Gadzooks, I've been homesick."

by evening,
Grandfather's teeth were still
nowhere to be found.

At dinner, Uncle Gaston
practiced shooting food out
of a cannon. Carl and Lefty
served while Grandfather
did the best he could without
his teeth.

after dinner, Mrs. Robinson read *Tarzan of the Apes* aloud. Suddenly, one of the frogs jumped up onto my hand and did a Tarzan yodel. *He was wearing Grandfather Robinson's teeth.*

"I found them! I found them!" I cried.

Everybody shouted, "Hooray!" except for Wilbur, who did a Tarzan yodel too.

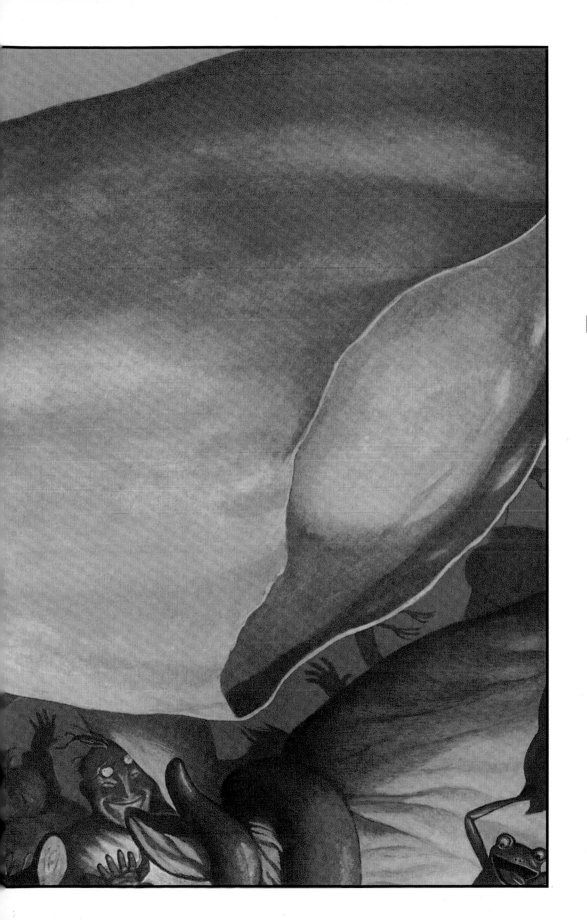

The occasion called for

a pillow fight.

exhausted from the battle, we floated across the lawn and into a tree with the help of Cousin Laszlo's antigravity device. Wilbur and I stayed up late into the night while Uncle Art told hair-raising stories about his adventures in outer space as the frogs played softly on their violins.

he next morning, the whole family gathered to wave good-bye, singing "Yes, We Have No Bananas," just like they always do.

I was kind of sad to leave, but I was ready to go home for a while.

"Good-bye, Wilbur," I said.

"Sorry it was such a dull day," Wilbur apologized.

"Hey, I had fun," I said. Wilbur smiled.

the sun was shining brightly as I walked slowly away.

I looked back over my shoulder, and there was Wilbur,

shooting himself out of Uncle Gaston's cannon with a

farewell message:

For John Henderson Cade—

a matchless pal and Robinson to the core

𝒜
atheneum

ATHENEUM BOOKS FOR YOUNG READERS

An imprint of Simon & Schuster Children's Publishing Division

1230 Avenue of the Americas, New York, New York 10020

Copyright © 1990, 2006 by William Joyce

Originally published in 1990 by Laura Geringer Books/HarperCollins Publishers

ATHENEUM BOOKS FOR YOUNG READERS is a registered trademark of Simon & Schuster, Inc.

Atheneum logo is a trademark of Simon & Schuster, Inc.

For information about special discounts for bulk purchases, please contact Simon & Schuster

Special Sales at 1-866-506-1949 or business@simonandschuster.com.

The Simon & Schuster Speakers Bureau can bring authors to your live event. For more

information or to book an event, contact the Simon & Schuster Speakers Bureau at

1-866-248-3049 or visit our website at www.simonspeakers.com.

Book design by Alicia Mikles

The text for this book was set in Futura BT.

The illustrations for this book were rendered in oil and acrylic.

Manufactured in China

0217 SCP

First Atheneum Books for Young Readers Edition

2 4 6 8 10 9 7 5 3 1

CIP data for this book is available from the Library of Congress.

ISBN 978-1-4814-8951-5

ISBN 978-1-4814-8952-2 (eBook)